BLACK SCREEN

                    FELIX(v.o)
          Joan,let not deceive ourselves,you
          and i know this is not working
          anymore,I have tried my best to keep
          it on,but I don't see this going
          anywhere,we just have to end this now
          before we hurt ourselves further,here
          is the divorce papers,please sign it
          and let move on

          JOAN(v.o)
               (nervous tone)
          No,Felix, don't do this,remember your
          vow,for better for worse

                    FELIX(v.o)
          and that was a mistake,I thought it
          was all rosy than thorn,but all I see
          is thorn,I can't even find rose,
          please help me out here, just do the
          needful and let go our separate ways

We hear the door squeak

                    JOAN(v.o)
               (Call out)
          Felix,Felix!!

We hear door slam

                    FADE IN:

EXT.ROAD.NIGHT

Close up on Francis, heavily drunk, driving on the lonely
dark road

He drinks from bottle he is holding

                    VOICE ON THE CAR RADIO
          Does true love exist,many people
          believe that true love doesn't
          exist,they believe that what we
          experience for our partner is
          obsession and relationship is just a
          game of fun,I would say this belief
          is why most relationship have hit the
          rock today, everyone afraid of being
          the victim in their
          relationship,rather they play
          around,in a theory I call,being the
          tough one,but my question is, the
          feeling of love is an emotion which
          is triggered by hormone action in the
          body,hormone that can change the
          psychology and be barely
          controlled,does it mean that who
          actually have this theory of playing
          around,do they have dead hormones or
          they just trying to suppress it,that
          could be hard you know.....

Felix phone rings

He turns off the radio,

Felix picks up the call

                    FELIX
               (Turn off the radio)
          I have tried,the truth is that,it is
          not working anymore,I am tired ,I
          just want to be alone, marriage is
          not for me,I can't handle the stress
          or task of marriage, marriage was one
          mistake I made,I am sorry if this
          hurt you all in anyway, it's the end
          for me

Felix cut the call

He pours all content of the drink into his mouth

He suddenly sees figure lying in the middle of the road

He swerve the car immediately roughly and crashes into the
bush

                    BLACK SCREEN

INT.MUDHUT.FOREST.MORNING

we fade in to a blurry vision of an old man staring down

We see felix sit up nervously, on a worn-out bed on the
ground

                    FELIX
              (curious)
         where am I,where am I?

Felix glancing around

The interior shows it is a mud hut,

The room is old,dirty and untidy,,

We see old potrait on the wall,mostly of a particular
lady(Monalisa)

Dirty and old kitchen utensil at the corner,

A desk and chair by entrance,

A fire lantern on the wall

Books litters everywhere

                    OLD MAN
              (walking to the corner of the
              house)
         Relax,you are safe here

The old man pick up a keg,pour it content into a cup,

We see Felix,hold his forehead,groan a bit in pain

Old man walk back to Felix,give him the cup

                    OLD MAN
         this will make you feel better

Felix take the cup,drinking from it suspiciously

The old man walk outside,

Felix drops the cup ,still nervous, observing the room

                                        CUT TO:

EXT.MUDHUT.FOREST.AFTERNOON

we drift round the trees,

Sun scorching , managing to reveal amid the trees

we hear bird chirping,

We now focus on the overview of the mud hut amid trees

In the space we can see oldman squatting over a firespot,in
front of the mud hut,

We zoom slowly to see him roasting yam

Francis walk out from the hut,still curious

Standing by the entrance to the hut,he stare at the the
oldman for a moment in silence

                    FELIX
              (Break the silence)
         how did I get here?

The oldman backing felix,glance at Felix, stands up and walk
to the corner of the hut,

He pick up Felix's whiskey lying on the ground

                    OLDMAN
              (sarcastic)
         why will a grown responsible man like
         you,be getting drunk, while
         driving,you could have gotten
         yourself or someone else killed,you
         know

The oldman open the whiskey and drink from it,

He bend over to the firespot, checking the yam

Felix continue watching in silence

                                        CUT TO:

EXT.MUDHUT.FOREST.EVENING

A long shot to see Felix and the oldman sitting on a bench
in front of the hut,eating the roasted yam in silence

Close up on Felix

                    FELIX
         so,for how long have you been here?

                    OLDMAN
         I can't remember,over 50 years,maybe

                    5.

Felix choke on the food,

                    FELIX
          You mean,you have been living in this
          forest for 50 years!

                    OLDMAN
          Yes, what is wrong with that!

                    FELIX
          It is weird!, especially in this
          modern days,where there are a lot to
          explore out there

The oldman grins

They eat in silence for a moment, finishing the last slice

                    FELIX
               (breaks silence)
          so,what about wife?

                    OLDMAN
               (Curious)
          what wife?

                    FELIX
          I saw her painting all over!!

                    OLDMAN
               (Stand up)
          There was and there is no wife!

          The oldman pick up the plate and walk
          into the hut

Close up on felix, looking so eager

                                        CUT TO:

INT.MUDHUT.FOREST.NIGHT

We focus Oldman sitting, writing on the desk,Using a fire
lantern for clear vision

A close up on his face to see his spetacles on

We now close up on felix face,staring at something

A medium shot on Felix to see him actually staring the Lady
(Monalisa) potrait on the wall

                    FRANCIS
          this art are really beautiful,the
          artist must have been drawing off
          heart or from a fantasy because there
          are slight difference, but you can
          tell it is the same person

We see the oldman engross in his writing, ignoring felix

                    FELIX
          for you to have her potrait
          everywhere,you must have missed her
          dearly,who is she to you!,a daughter?

                    OLDMAN
               (Feeling irritated)
          You ask too much question, don't you
          think of going to your wife?

                    FELIX
               (Curious)
          how do you know I am Married

                    OLDMAN
               (still writing)
          there's a ring on your finger

Francis check his finger to see the ring

                    OLDMAN
          she must be worried,you know

                    FRANCIS
               (still staring at the finger)
          well,I can't go home

                    OLD MAN
               (Still writing)
          why?

                         FRANCIS
          I am getting divorce

Close up on the oldman as he chuckles

                    OLDMAN
               (writing)
          Children of nowadays

Felix turn to the oldman

                          7.

                    FELIX
          This is not a matter of time
          difference,it is an emotions,the
          concept of true love doesn't exist,
          what we experience is obsession,your
          ability to endure through, is what
          make your relationship last, true
          love doesn't exist

                    OLDMAN
          you think so

                    FELIX
          I know so

                    OLDMAN
          you probably must have read love
          story like.....

                    FELIX
                 (Interrupt)
          Oh yes,like Romeo and Juliet,jack and
          rose,titanic,all this are not even
          real life story ,they are created
          from the writers fantasy,

Oldman drops his writing and focus on felix

                    OLDMAN
          well,I have a real one for you

Francis sit on the bed

                    OLDMAN
          it all started in a small
          province,during military regime in
          1974......

                                                          CUT TO:
          EXT.GENERAL BASSEY BASE.DAY

we transition to an overview of four soldier,CAPTAIN
MACAULAY,30, and   3 others, standing shoulder to shoulder,
dressed in dark green khaki and shirt,each carrying a riffle
on their shoulder,in front an old model storey building

Still focus on the soldiers,we see an old model Mercedes
Benz drives in,

It stops in front of the waiting soldiers

                    OLDMAN (V.O)
          there was once a general,let me say,a
          deadly general

We close up on the GENERAL BASSEY'S leg steps out of the
car,

We drift from the leg to the full body to reveal GENERAL
BASSEY,50, a built, fierce looking man dressed in high rank
military uniform,heavy moustache,afrohair

Captain Macaulay and three other soldiers salute him,

He ignores them, glancing around sternly

Still focus on general bassey we can see,
MONALISA,25,dressed in Ankara and top,Ankara headtie,
alighting from the other side of the car

The three soldier hurries to the back of the car, offloading
luggage from the car to the house,

we see captain Macaulay still standing in front of general
Macaulay,now lead the way into the house,

General bassey and Monalisa follows him

                                              CUT TO:

INT.SITTING ROOM.GENERAL BASSEY BASE.CONTINUOUS

we focus Monalisa face,admiring something on the wall

Over Monalisa's shoulder,We can see general bassey and
Captain macualay far off,in mute discussion

The interior decor and appliance of a classic 90's model,

The three soldier still gallivanting, carrying luggages to
the interior

We focus on Monalisa backing the screen staring at art
potrait on the wall

General bassey walk to view,pat Monalisa

                    GENERAL BASSEY
          classique,right,you see I know
          exactly your taste in art,so I made
          sure,the best and top-notch artwork
          were erected here to meet your
          taste!!

Monalisa ignores general bassey,still staring at the
portrait

                    GENERAL BASSEY
          well,I see you are already falling
          love with them already,I can request
          for more,if you wish, you see,all I
          just want is to make sure you are in
          the right frame of mind,you know your
          happiness is my priority,

General bassey trying to peck Monalisa,

Monalisa wave her head to shoves him off,

General bassey pauses,then smiles

He soothes Monalisa shoulder and walk away from her

                    MONALISA
          you said,I will practice here!!!

                    GENERAL BASSEY
               (walking to the interior)
          well,I have forgotten that too!

We close up on Monalisa now admiring the portrait

                    FADE OUT;

INT.HAKEEM'S HOUSE.ROOM.MORNING

we focus on the clock on the wall,8:28am

we drift round the poorly furnished,90's model interior to
see spilled art paint, drawing board,scattered clothes,
books,dirty dishes,unfinished portrait,

Potrait on the wall,a mirror on the wall

A chair and desk,on the desk are books,radio,a cup
containing biro , toothbrush and comb

We now focus on HAKEEM 28 and ADDO,28, sleeping on the worn-
out bed and snoring heavily,

We see Hakeem,afro hair, heavy moustache,struggling to wake
up, finally,sit up, still sleepy,he stretches him,soon his
eyes catch the clock on the wall, 8:33am,

He jumps off the bed immediately, nervous

he gallivants in confusion,Eventually Picks up a toothbrush from the desk,

Hurriedly walking away he mistakenly kick a paint container, spilling it's content,

                    HAKEEM
               (murmuring)
          gosh!!!

He ignores the paint and hurries out of the house,

Soon we see him walk in,his face wet with water,

We focus on his hands dropping the toothbrush In the container of toothbrush

we focus on Addo still snoring heavily

Hakeem picks up a bucket from the corner of the house, walking away,

He seem irritated by addo snoring

He picks up a pillow,hit it on addo,

                    HAKEEM
          Huh!!

Addo still sleeping,

Hakeem walk out of the room

                                             CUT TO:

EXT.HAKEEM'S HOUSE.ROOM.CONTINUOUS

we focus on Hakeem reflection on the mirror,

Hakeem spectacle on,

He combs his moustache and hair,as he stare at the mirror on the wall, whistling

We still hears addo snoring heavily

Hakeem admires himself in the mirror,picks up his Papa's cap from the desk beside,wear it on,

 He picks up a book and cane from the desk and walk out of the room

                                             CUT TO:

EXT.HAKEEM'S HOUSE.CONTINUOUS

we focus on an overview of old model bungalow,amid typical 1990's average compound

A bicycle by the side of the building

We see Hakeem walking out of the house, whistling,as he picks up the bicycle and rides off

                                                    CUT TO:

EXT.DUSTY ROAD.DAY

Close up on hakeem's bicycle wheel as it rolls,

Now an overview of Hakeem on his bicycle riding on the dusty road

                                                    CUT TO:

EXT.SCHOOL.CONTINUOUS

We see Hakeem packing his bicycle by a tree

Ahead is a dilapidated school buildings

We can see disorganize and noisy class ahead of hakeem

Hakeem head toward the classroom

                                                    CUT TO:

INT.CLASSROOM.CONTINUOUS

The class still noisy,

The student 15-17 chattering and laughing heavily,

 some sitting inappropriate on the desk,some gallivanting about

Zoom in and close up on hakeem, standing in front of the class,

Student ignorant of his present

We close up on Hakeem as he clears his voice,

                    HAKEEM
               (screams)
          shut up!!!

The class is now calm and quiet,

They sit properly

Hakeem stare at them furiously

                    HAKEEM
                 (Gallivanting)
           nincompoop,bambozu!!,idiot!,
           porcupine, monkey!!!,

we focus on one of the student giggling

Hakeem turns to her,

She cut her giggling, straighten her face immediately

                    HAKEEM
               (Still staring at her)
           why are you laughing?,do I look like
           a comedian!,answer me!

The girl nods sideway

                    HAKEEM
           so tell me, what is amusing you?,

The student head down innocently

                    HAKEEM
           ,I am talking to you,and you still
           sitting

The student stands up

 Hakeem stare at her sternly for moment

                    HAKEEM
           look at your head,coconus nucifera!

We see the class laughing

                    HAKEEM
                (Shun the class)
           Heey!!!

The class calm

                    HAKEEM
           why are you laughing?,I am shunning
           someone for laughing,yet you all
           still doing this same,if I ask
           now,what coconus nucifera is,neither
           of you can say it,infact,

Hakeem point at one of the pupil

                    HAKEEM
          Hey,you,what is coconus nucifera

The boy hesitate

                    HAKEEM
          I am not suprise you don't know it,

He point to the next,

                    HAKEEM
          what is coconus nucifera?

The next person hesitate

                    HAKEEM
          remain standing,

He point to another person

The person hesitate

                    HAKEEM
          Wait,so none of you knows what that
          means,and you were all laughing

Hakeem chuckles

Hakeem walk to the board and write " coconus nucifera",

                    HAKEEM
          this is an assignment for you
          all,find the meaning of the words and
          attach it to your name,all of you,in
          the mean time,you all should stand
          till class end,.

The class murmuring,as they stands up

                    HAKEEM
          shut up!!!

Close up on hakeem face,

He turns to write on the board

                    CUT TO:

INT.SISTER DORCAS OFFICE.MISSIONARY HEALTH CENTER.DAY

we focus on Christ potrait on the wall

                    SISTER DORCAS(O.S)
          you,see,you need to be taking much
          fruit,it will help build up your
          child bone and immune system,also you
          need to stay hydrated and exercise
          all the time,it is crucial for a
          pregnant mother,so here is your
          drugs,the prescription are inside the
          pack,follow them religiously

we drift to see the full interior,an average old model
office

we focus on SISTER DORCAS,50,a woman dressed in Reverend
sister attire, spetacles on,giving a pregnant woman sitting
in front of her a package

                    PREGNANT WOMAN
          thank you sister!

Pregnant woman stand up and walk to the door and open

General bassey and Monalisa walk in as the pregnant woman
walk away,

                    SISTER DORCAS
               (stand up)
          oh!!!, general bassey,you are welcome

General bassey sit rudely

                    MONALISA
               (sitting)
          good morning sister!

                    SISTER DORCAS
               (Smiling)
          It is a pleasure to have the general
          at my office such a beautiful morning

We see general bassey take out a cigarette and lit it,he
puff out smoke

                    GENERAL BASSEY
          well,not here for Courtesy,you see my
          queen will be assisting in the
          center,so you should make an
          available space immediately for her

Monalisa glance at general bassey

                    SISTER DORCAS
          Oh!,that is great, absolutely,you see
          I have been doing this alone
          here,since the last missionary helper
          ,Mrs Flora,a white lady, left to
          britain with her husband,an
          assistance here is so much
          appreciated, especially that of a
          general wife,it will attract more eye
          and donation to the missionary,when
          do you wish to start

                    MONALISA
               (smiling)
          as soon as possible,ma!

General bassey engross on his smoking

                    SISTER DORCAS
          May the God Lord bless you my
          daughter, The community will be so
          happy to have you and.....

                    GENERAL BASSEY
               (interrupt)
          What is the security here like?

                    SISTER DORCAS
               (Curious)
          security?,well,we haven't recorded
          any security issue in the
          community,let alone a hospital

                    GENERAL BASSEY
          I am talking of security against male
          counterpart, dummy!

                    MONALISA
               (Cautioning)
          Bassey!

                    SISTER DORCAS
          Sir,I don't understand...

Monalisa stand and walk away aggressively

General bassey draws closer, staring at sister Dorcas, blows
smoke to her face

Sister dorcas takes her face away

                        GENERAL BASSEY
              you see,Monalisa is my gold,a
              precious gold I cherish so much,and i
              don't want anyone toying with my gold
              while I am not watching,so for as
              long as she works here with you,you
              have to watch her closer and keep her
              for me,you get it now

Sister Dorcas in stun

General bassey draw back,grins and stand up and walk out of
the office

Sister Dorcas display sign of the cross,and sighs

                                                  CUT TO:

EXT.ROAD.DAY

Inside the motion general bassey mercedez benz

We see captain macaulay on the steering

General bassey and Monalisa sitting at the back seat both
looking opposite sides

Close up on Monalisa face

DREAM SEQUENCE BEGINS

EXT.RIVERSIDE.DAY

(SCENE IN BLACK AND WHITE

we zoom out to see an overview of Monalisa sitting on a
chair on Riverbank surrounded by thick forestation,

She smiling and posing

now we drift back to see an overview of Hakeem standing in
front of her painting her potrait on a drawing board

We zoom back to Monalisa face

DREAM SEQUENCE ENDS

                                                  CUT TO:

INT.HAKEEM'S ROOM.DAY

Close up on Hakeem as he sit up from a sleep

He observes around,

He covers his face in disappointment, groans a bit

He now sigh,get off the bed to the exterior

CUT TO:

EXT.RIVERSIDE.DAY

we drift round the trees,

We can hear bird chirping,

We can hear an unclear of a football commentator on the
radio

We now focus on the flowing river,

we focus on a radio,

The sound from the radio becomes louder

Now we focus on a chair in front of river

we drift backward to see hakeem, glancing continually at the
chair and painting on a half paint portrait of
Monalisa,beside him the radio on the ground

Close up on him,as he pauses for moment, close his eyes in
meditation,

He opens his eyes,

He drops the brush aggressively to the ground,

Focus on the brush touching the ground beside the radio

CUT TO:

EXT.ROAD.EVENING

overview of hakeem riding on a bicycle, holding the potrait
on his arm,his radio tied to the bicycle backseat

Soon we see addo's van, riding close to him,

Hakeem stops his bicycle

The van stops,engine still on

We close up on Addo on the steering,

                    ADDO
          Hakeem, my friend,I can see you are
          coming from the stream,to draw your
          imaginary wife,mammy water!

                    HAKEEM
               (pissed off)
          did I tell you that?

                    ADDO
          it is obvious,you don't need to tell
          me,when did you start drawing for
          commercial purpose,that you will be
          carrying portrait around,i must tell
          you,this is really turning to
          madness,soon now we will hear that
          you are now roaming the street
          naked,imagine,someone will wake up
          from sleep,go to Riverside and start
          drawing image of someone he is not
          sure if she exist!

                    HAKEEM
          And how is that your business,addo!

                    ADDO
          it is my business ooh, because if you
          start running mad,I will be the one
          running about to find the cure,so
          prevention is better than cure

                    HAKEEM
               (Retaliating)
          is you that will run mad

                    ADDO
          what I pity most,is your dying
          bicycle,you keep stressing the poor
          thing

                    HAKEEM
          what about your car,it is also worn
          out, can't you see

                    ADDO
          come on,you can't compare a bicycle
          to car,no matter the state it is,a
          car is always better than a bicycle

                    HAKEEM
          that is a lie

                    ADDO
          you don't need argue with me,you know
          the truth,look at you sweating like a
          he-goat,from peddling,infact hop
          in,let me show the wonder of a van,

Hakeem hisses and continue peddling

                    ADDO
          look at someone I want to
          help,well,it is ok, continue
          suffering

Addo accelerate the car

                                        CUT TO:

EXT.ROAD.CONTINOUS

Another section of the road

we focus on Hakeem peddling his bicycle forcefully and
tiredly

Behind we see addo van riding and meeting up with him

Both still in motion

                    ADDO
          come on,stop forming hard guy,hop
          in,I know you are already tired from
          peddling

Hakeem stops his bicycle,hesitate then get off the bicycle,

he carries the bicycle and drop it at the back of the van

Hakeem enters the car

                    HAKEEM
               (cautioning)
          I need to warn again, don't ever
          insult my means of transportation
          again

                    ADDO
          Your means of transportation is
          already insulting itself and it's
          owner already,so I don't need to heap
          insult again,

                    HAKEEM
          Even if, i don't want hear it
          anymore.

                    ADDO
          wait are you challenging me,do you
          want to go down from the car?

                    HAKEEM
          please move the car!

                    ADDO
          speak to me politely,my friend!

Addo accelerate the car

                                             CUT TO:

EXT.ROAD.CONTINOUS

another section of the road,

An overview of the van coming to a stop,

Close up on Addo and Hakeem in the van

                         ADDO
                    (murmuring)
          ooooh,not again!!

                         HAKEEM
                    (curious)
          what is wrong?

                    ADDO
          please,you will do something for
          me,can you help me push the car a bit
          please,

                    HAKEEM
          Like seriously?, and you were
          insulting my bicycle

                    ADDO
          But my van is still better than your
          bicycle,

                    HAKEEM
          if you talk more than your mouth
          now,I will abandon you here

                    ADDO
               (Apologizing)
          Ok,I am sorry,please just help me out

Hakeem alight from the car

He walk to the back of the van and start pushing it

We focus Addo controlling the steering

Back to Hakeem pushing the car fiercely

                                                    CUT TO:

EXT.ROAD.CONTINUOUS

The day getting dark

Another section of the road,

We see Hakeem still pushing the car, sweating profusely

He stops pushing and walk to Hakeem

                    HAKEEM
          What exactly is wrong with the car,

                    ADDO
          I don't really know,I think it is the
          engine or something,please push it a
          little bit it will start this time I
          promise

We focus on Hakeem walk to the back of the van bicycle,
Take out his bicycle and climb on

                    ADDO
               (Glance back)
          push it harder please

Addo sight Hakeem about riding off

He alight immediately

                    ADDO
               (Walk to Hakeem)
          Hakeem,what are you doing?

                    HAKEEM
          What does it look like I am doing?

                    ADDO
          I asked you to push the car

                    HAKEEM
          do i look like your servant,it is
          your cross,carry it, wonder of a car
          indeed,

Hakeem rides off

Addo groans in anger,

He kicks his car continually,then stops

He walk to the bonnet,open and cross check,

He gallivants about in confusion,

He then sit on the ground, leaning by car in dejection

                                              CUT TO:
                                       EXT.ROAD.DAY

we close up on addo sleeping inside the stationary car at
the same spot

He wake up,to sees kids chattering, walking along the road

He alight the car immediately

                    ADDO
                  (Waving)
            Heeey,heey, please come!

We see the kids walking toward him

                                              CUT TO:

EXT.HAKEEM'S HOUSE.MORNING

we see the kids pushing the car into the compound

At the same,hakeem fully dressed in corporate, holding a
book and cane,rides out on his bicycle, ignoring the
activities

Addo wave to the kids

The kids stops pushing and run off

Addo comes out the car,walk aggressively into the house.

                                              CUT TO:

EXT.SCHOOL.DAY

we focus on Hakeem gallivanting the organized class

We drift round the classroom

                    HAKEEM (CONT'D)
               (Teaching)
          Transportation is a mean of moving
          goods and person from one place to
          another,there are different medium of
          transportation, either by water,air
          and land,and for those of you who
          believes in fetish means,you can add
          teleporting,oh I forget,you all have
          myopic iq,I mean transportation by
          air,water,land and juju'

The class laughs

                    HAKEEM
          the most common means of
          transportation everywhere is
          original, natural way,leg or let me
          say walking,and mainly in today world
          especially Western world we have
          car,train, Ship and airplane, common
          in Africa,we have camel,
          horse,donkey, canoe and juju,in
          quote, plantain leaf

The class laughs again

                    HAKEEM
          although,some of the Western means of
          transportation are gaining popularity
          in Africa system, especially
          vehicles,few of us are privilege to
          have it to aid their movement,and
          some also have it to delay their
          journey and cause them stagnancy,do
          you all understand what I mean by
          that?

The class yells no"

                    HAKEEM
          then,that is an assignment for you
          all

The class murmuring

                    HAKEEM
               (ignores the murmuring)
          you all are going to list out 10 ways
          in which a vehicle can delay and
          cause stagnancy in transportation
          circle,in other word list 10
          disadvantage of Western means of
          transportation in Africa,bye for now

Hakeem walk out of the class

The student now chattering, murmuring preparing to leave the class

                                        CUT TO:

INT.HAKEEM'S HOUSE.DAY

IN THE KITCHEN

we open on a poorly furnish kitchen,

We can see dirty kitchen utensil

We see addo walking into the kitchen, yawning,

He open one of the pot on the stove curiously

In the dirty pot is a paper with a text " sweet rice"

Addo hisses in aggression,and swipe the pot down from the stove,

He walk out of the kitchen

IN THE ROOM

we see addo walk in from the kitchen

He walk to the desk,take out a tape and put it in the radio,he turn it on,

GENTLEMAN BY FELA ANIKULAPO KUTI PLAYING

addo Fling himself to bed,head up in thought,

high angle shot on Addo laying on bed staring at the ceiling

                                        CUT TO:

EXT.GENERAL BASSEY'S OFFICE.DAY

we close up on a map on the desk,

Overview of general bassey and Captain macualay cross checking the map,
                CAPTAIN MACAULAY
        All this region marked already, starting from the
northwest axis to Southern axis,they are all paying their
taxes concurrent to province purse which is under our
control, as instructed by the former regime before your
turn,

                    GENERAL BASSEY
               (point a region in the map)
          what about this region, not marked

                    CAPTAIN MACAULAY
          That is the ngali tribe region,they
          are very sacred people,often referred
          to be the heart of the province,so
          over the past regime they have been
          exempted from tax, in respect of
          their sacredness,so they are
          sovereign

                    GENERAL BASSEY
          what is their major produces?

                    CAPTAIN MACAULAY
          Well,major producers of palm and
          cocoa product,but mainly known for
          palm export especially,they supply to
          about 10 provinces....

                    GENERAL BASSEY
               (Interrupt)
          I want them under my regime,

                    CAPTAIN MACAULAY
          but sir.....

                    GENERAL BASSEY
          no but!,my orders should reach them
          as soon as possible,I need them to
          pay taxes to me,

We see captain Macaulay salutes general bassey

                    CAPTAIN MACAULAY
               yes,sir

Captain Macualay walk out of the office,

Close up on general bassey,takes out a cigarette and lit it

                                             CUT TO:

EXT.NGALI.DAY

An establishing shot to show an overview of a typical
village center,mud housing system scatters around

INTERSWITCHING SCENE

1) A MAN HARVEST PALM PRODUCT FROM THE TREE

2) CHILDREN PLAYING CLAPPING GAME UNDER A TREE IN THE
VILLAGE SQUARE

3) WOMAN FRYING GRAIN IN KIOSK KITCHEN

4) A WOMAN SERVING FOOD TO AN OLD MAN SITTING IN FRONT OF A
HUT

5)AT THE KING PROVINCE,WE SEE 3 ELDER SITTING ON THE GROUND,
CONJURING,FORMING A CHAMBER ROUND A KING,STILL ON WHITE
WRAPPER AND BARE CHEST,

                    A TRADITIONALIST PERFORM RITUAL ON
                    HIM
          6) A YOUNG MAIDEN,OMA,19 AND REST
          CARRYING WATER POT, CHATTERING AS
          THEY WALK DOWN THE BUSHY PATH

                    CUT TO;

EXT.VILLAGE PATH.DAY

we close up drunkard lying on the bush,eyes closed,his
bicycle and keg lying beside him,

A troops van conveying Captain Macaulay and his men drive
pass him

He sit up immediately in curiosity,

He glances at the vehicle for a moment

He picks up his keg and bicycle,and rides out

                                        CUT TO:

EXT.PALACE SQUARE.NGALI.CONTINUOUS

The king,elder and traditonalist still engross on the ritual
exercise,

We drift to see two able bodied guard at the entrance

The rituals on the Kings still on,

Long shot to see the drunkard riding in on his bicycle,
screaming

                    DRUNKARD
               (Riding in, screaming)
          they are coming!,they are coming!!

The drunkard jump off his bicycle about running in,is
stopped by two guard

                    DRUNKARD
               (Persisting)
          They are coming!!!

The attention of the king and the rest turn to the drunkard

                    KING
               (Stand up,in curiosity)
          who is coming!!!

                    DRUNKARD
               (Drunk tone)
          Troops, heavily armed troops,they are
          about to invade us,we are finished!!

                    ELDER1
          he is drunk!

                    KING
          Mr Man,do you realize,a serious
          business is going on here and you
          come here to display your drunken
          act!!

                    DRUNKARD
          no,I am saying the truth,I saw them
          with my eyes.

                    KING
               (to the guard)
          Take him away,

                    DRUNKARD
               (Persisting)
          I am saying the truth

The guard in attempt to whisk off the drunkard

The troop van drives in,

Everyone stares in curiosity

Captain Macaulay and two armed soldier jump off the van,

They walk toward the king

The guard stops them with their spear,

The military men glances at the guard scornfully,

Captain Macualay stare at the king

                28.

                    CAPTAIN MACAULAY
          You have been asked to submit to the
          regime of general bassey,chief
          commandant of westside province,that
          you will abide by its Constitutional
          laws and orders and all taxes from
          your production be paid to and only
          him,and he also will be overseeing
          the activities of the region

The king glances at his elders and they all burst to
laughter

                    KING
               (Turn to captain Macualay)
          Is this a joke or something,the
          ancient region of ngali has been a
          sovereign region only to be ruled by
          monarchy,many top generals has
          accepted and respected the fact, here
          a general from nowhere,want to come
          and claim it all of a sudden,it is so
          ridiculous!

The king and his men laughs again

                    CAPTAIN MACAULAY
          you have till your village next
          market to respond and failure to do
          so,will lead to consequencial
          actions,

                    KING
          and you,go and tell your general,that
          I,ozobialla,will bow and submit to no
          general and life or death!!!,

The elder cheers the king

Captain Macaulay order his men to the van and drives off

The king and his elders goes back to their Ritual
activities,

The drunkard picks up his bicycle and rides off

                                             CUT TO:

EXT.HALL.MISSIONARY HEALTH CENTRE.DAY

We focus on Monalisa standing infront sitting elderly men
and women

                    MONALISA
          Ageing comes with different
          symptom,to some,they may experience
          poor vision or hearing,some, hair
          loss,others experience memory loss,or
          let me use forgetful, mostly for
          all,we see skin wrinkling and
          sagging,ageing is actually a good
          thing and a privilege,you all can
          testify that too,so at old age,they
          are some step you need to take to
          help improve your healthy
          living,first of all,staying
          happy,healthy diet and staying
          fit,spend quality time with those you
          love and avoid stress and
          overthinking,check for your BP and
          sugar level always and...

                                        FADE TO:

INT.SISTER DORCAS OFFICE.MISSIONARY HEALTH CENTER.DAY

Monalisa sitting,facing sister dorcas

                    SISTER DORCAS
          You see the Lord have given the
          spirit to fight and not to faint,you
          have to be strong,if not for anything
          but for the future, because I see a
          bright future for you,forget the past
          or the present,just pray and believe
          it should fade away,no matter how
          tough it is

We close up on Monalisa bowing her head

                                        CUT TO:

EXT.COMPOUND.EVENING

We open on poor old model compound,

Dilaidated building,

In the space,we see addo van,loaded with logs

An elderly man and addo beside the van

one of Hakeem pupil,ARIN,15,at the corner sitting on a bench
, writing

                    ELDERLY MAN
              (counting the wood in the van)
         one,two three,four,five,six....

                    ADDO
              (Cut in)
         It is complete

                    ELDERLY MAN
         complete right,

                    ADDO
         Yes, complete

elderly man pat addo on the shoulder

Addo enter his van,

              ELDERLY MAN
         drive safe,my son

Arin stand from her seat and walk to addo

                    ARIN
         sir, wait!

Addo stare at her curiosity

                    ARIN
         can I ask a question?

                    ADDO
         go on,my dear

                    ARIN
         Can vehicle hinder transportation?

Addo smiles

                    ADDO
         No,my dear, vehicle doesn't hinder
         transportation,they only aid
         Transportation and make it easier,if
         not for my vehicle,I can't help your
         father carry this load around,so it
         doesn't hinder transportation at all

                    ARIN
         but,our teacher said vehicles delay
         transportation,

                    ADDO
         really?

                    31.

                    ARIN
          Yes,he even asked us to give 10 ways
          vehicle can hinder transportation

                    ADDO
          what is your name,my dear

                    ARIN
          Arin

                    ADDO
          Arin,your teacher might probably be
          playing around,vehicle can never
          hinder transport,your teacher might
          be angered for not having or does he
          have one?

                    ARIN
          no,Mr Hakeem doesn't have one

                    ADDO
             (suprise)
          did you say Mr Hakeem

                    ARIN
          yes, that is my teacher name

Addo sighs deeply

                    ADDO
          you see my dear,vehicle were invented
          by the white to help us in our day to
          day activities,the white who created
          it,knows it is for our betterment
          that why they created it, don't
          listen to what some jealous people
          say to you,ok,when they tell you
          something is not good,tell them to
          acquire one and check for it's
          importance,ok

Arins nods

Addo ignite the car,

Arin walk away

Addo drives off

                                        CUT TO:

INT.GENERAL'S OFFICE.DAY

we focus on general sitting relax to his chair, smoking,
twirling a pen between his fingers,in meditation

                    CAPTAIN MACAULAY(o.s)
             so,what are we going to do now,

We close up on captain Macaulay, sitting before general
bassey

General bassey still twirling the pen in meditation,

General bassey stops twirling,break the pen to half fiercely

He then takes one half,and sign on a paper

He hands it to captain Macaulay,

Captain Macualay glances through the paper and grins,

He salute general bassey and walk away.

Close up on general bassey face looking furious

                                        FADE TO:

EXT.VILLAGE SQUARE.NGALI.NIGHT

we open on a controversial village setting,

A bonfire

We hear drumming

We see a young teen boy,pouring gin to a deities at the
corner of a hut

Far off,we see kids playing clapping game,

We also young maidens dancing to a drummer tune,

While a woman serving the elders, sitting in circle,
chattering and laughing,

The activities continues,

Soon we see captain macualay troops van drive in
roughly,stop abruptly,

They fires to the air,

Everyone panics, scampering for safety,

The troops ambush them,

We see the young teen boy, drops the gin bottle and run off,

The troops,orders everyone to lies forcefully

We drift round to see the villager laying on the
ground,panics and wailing

The troops molesting them, brutally

                                        CUT TO:

EXT.VILLAGE PATH.DAY.

Ground level shot to see the young teen boy running
fiercely,panting heavily

                                        CUT TO:

EXT.KING'S PROVINCE.CONTINUOUS

The villagers lying on the ground , wailing

The troops molesting them,

Soon we see the troops picking out,the maidens,one by one to
the vans,

Everyone sobbing,

The troops shunning them

Soon,the troops orders the elder to kneel down,

About shooting them,

We see a woman blocking them,

They shoot the woman dead

Everyone wailing loudly

                                        CUT TO:

EXT.KING'S PROVINCE.CONTINUOUS

We see the king,standing outside curious,on hearing the
villagers village

We see two guard standing beside him,

the wailing increasing

The traditionalist sitting on the ground conjuring

                    KING
                 (curious)
           what could be wrong?

Wail still on,

We see the young teen boy,runs in panting

                    YOUNG TEEN BOY
           your highness,they are killing us

                    KING
           who?

Close up on the young teen boy,panting heavily,hesitate to
speak, pointing behind

We hear gunshot,

The boy fall dead to the ground to reveal captain Macaulay
and another soldier,

The guard about attacking them,

Captain Macaulay shoot them dead,

The troops whisk the king and traditionalist away.

                                        CUT TO:

EXT.VILLAGE SQUARE.NIGHT

we drift round corpses of the drummer,elders,woman and kids
litters the ground

The bonfire still burning

                    CUT TO:

EXT.VILLAGE PATH.MORNING

we focus on the king and traditionalist neck hangs dead
together to a tree

                                        CUT TO:

EXT.VILLAGE PATH.NGALI.MORNING

A ground level shot on the bush

The troop van conveying them with four maiden,drives into
view and away

                    FADE OUT:

           EXT.GENERAL BASSEY'S BASE.DAY

we open on Monalisa inside the halting car,watching general
bassey talking and demonstrating to the four maiden standing
helplessly before him,

Captain Macaulay,two other soldier stands beside him

Still on Monalisa POV, watching general bassey and the
maiden

soon the driver opens the door

She alight curiously,

We close on her face,

Close up on general bassey at stopping his speech staring
back at Monalisa

                    CUT TO:

INT.ROOM.GENERAL BASSEY'S BASE.CONTINUOUS

we see Monalisa sitting on the bed,head down in aggressive
mood,playing with finger

Soon the door opens,

General bassey enter

Monalisa stands up to general bassey aggressively

                    MONALISA
            what have you done?

                    GENERAL BASSEY
            what have I done?

                    MONALISA
            you destroy people's home and
            captured them as slave,and act like
            you have done nothing wrong,this
            people are humans also

                    GENERAL BASSEY
          well,I can treat them as I wish

                    MONALISA
               (Sarcastically)
          oh really?

                    GENERAL BASSEY
          yes,of course

                    MONALISA
          You are demon!!,heartless and evil

                    GENERAL BASSEY
               (pissed off)
          how dare you talk to me like that?

                    MONALISA
          yes,I will talk to you as I wish,
          anytime you display your evil act,do
          you know what it remind me of,all the
          time,how you destroyed my
          village,kill my people,my family
          especially and turn me to your slave

                    GENERAL BASSEY
          You are not my slave,you are my wife

Monalisa chuckles

                    MONALISA
          wife indeed,how do one get a
          wife,visit her kinsmen,do the
          traditonal rite,and claim her,but you
          took me hostage,and claim I am your
          wife,I don't even have freedom of my
          own,I can do or go anywhere except
          you permit,and you claim I am your
          wife,I rather die than to be a wife
          to a beast!!

General bassey raise his hand in attempt to slap Monalisa

Monalisa frights

General bassey stare at furiously for moment

                    GENERAL BASSEY
          don't you dare piss me off!!

Brings his hand down,walk away and slams the door

We see Monalisa groans in anger and cries aloud

                                        CUT TO:

EXT.FARM.DAY

A high angle shot to show an overview of the four maiden in the farm working,

Two of captain Macaulay soldier monitoring them

We see general bassey Mercedes Benz drives in,and halt

Monalisa comes down from the car,

She is carrying pack of clothes and a small cooler

She walk to one of the monitoring   soldier

                    MONALISA
            Assemble the girls

The soldier sign to the other soldier far off

The second soldier forcefully assembling the maiden

Monalisa gives him a shunning look,

The   nervous maiden assemble before Monalisa

Monalisa sighs

                    MONALISA
                (comforting)
        I can feel your pains,your agony,
        losing family, friends,loved one,
        community and above all being turn to
        slave,in very similar way,I am still
        experiencing the same as you all,but
        I don't want to talk about it,I just
        want to encourage you all to stay
        strong and fight, till you find your
        happiness and freedom again,we all
        are going to be free from the shackle
        one day,

Close on Monalisa face as she sighs

                    MONALISA
        I just brought clothes and food for
        you all,I know you will be needing
        them,so you should eat for now before
        you go back to your....

Focus on the maiden walking away one after the other
ignoring and rejecting Monalisa package,

They pick up their farm tools start working,

We see the soldiers about attacking them

                    MONALISA
              (Cautioning the soldiers)
          Hold it!

We focus on Monalisa watching at the maiden in despair,as
they work on the farm,

She carries her back to the car

The car drives off

Overview of girls working on the farm

                                                  CUT TO:

EXT.HAKEEM'S HOUSE.EVENING

we focus on Hakeem pushing his bicycle with a potrait to
the compound,

We can see addo van, stationary in the compound

In the verandah,addo sitting on the bench, panting his
feet,in aggression

Hakeem park his bicycle at the usual spot

He walk to the verandah

                    ADDO
              (Stand up)
          so,you went about telling your
          students,that my van is a hindrance
          to transportation,

                    HAKEEM
          isn't it?, wait,is that why you are
          panting like someone bitten by a
          monkey

                    ADDO
          does monkey bite?

                    HAKEEM
          you tell me,does it bite,

Addo hiss

                    ADDO
          how can you go about, telling kids,
          that my van is hinderance to
          transportation

                    HAKEEM
          You started it first,by insulting my
          bicycle,

                    ADDO
          obviously,your bicycle is the main
          hinderance to transportation,what is
          the difference between a peddling and
          trekking,both of them make use of
          leg, bicycle is just an advance means
          of trekking

                    HAKEEM
          atleast bicycle don't have knocked
          engine,that will cost lot of money to
          repair,beside a means of
          transportation that only not readily
          available to the low class is just an
          intimidation

                    ADDO
          Oh,thank God,you have classify
          yourself as a low class

                    HAKEEM
          and you think you are the high
          class,or have you forgotten,how you
          bought your van, should I start
          remind you,well I am just coming back
          from along journey,so I am very
          farmish

Hakeem walk inside

                    ADDO
          yeah,I left some food for you in the
          pot,go and eat

Addo smiles as he sit

                                        CUT TO:

INT.HAKEEM'S HOUSE.DAY

IN THE KITCHEN

we see Hakeem yawning,as he enters the kitchen,

                40.

The kitchen still untidy

Hakeem close his nose in irritation

He open the pot on the stove,

Focus on the pot,to see the letter inscription "sweet rice"

Hakeem chuckles and walk away

                                              CUT TO:

IN THE ROOM

we close up on hakeem lying,face up on the bed,

He stretch his hand to click on the radio beside him

OSONDI OWENDI BY OSADEBE PLAYING

 close up on hakeem face in meditation

                    HAKEEM(V.O)
               yesterday,we talk about
               transportation

                                              FADE TO:

INT.CLASSROOM.DAY

we transition to Hakeem standing in front of a class

                    HAKEEM
               Last week we talk about
               transportation Where I explain the
               meaning,medium and forms of
               transportation,I also gave an
               assignment, of which I got some
               report of some of you making
               research,and I am pretty sure,you all
               are ready to cite your founding,so
               who is going first,tell us the
               disadvantage of vehicles in
               Africa...

The classroom is silent,

                    HAKEEM
               Anyone?

The class still silent and calm

                    HAKEEM
          so,you mean none of you have a point?

We focus on Arin raising her

                    HAKEEM
          Yes,Arin,state your point

Arin stands up,sigh

                                             CUT TO:

EXT.SCHOOL.CONTINUOUS

An overview of addo van halting at the school compound

Addo alight from the car,

He proceed toward the Hakeem class

He caught a sight at Hakeem bicycle at an edge,

he grins and walk toward it

                                             CUT TO:

INT.CLASSROOM.CONTINUOUS

still focus on Arin

                    ARIN
          actually sir,I don't see any
          disadvantage in vehicles, basically
          vehicle were build to aid our
          transportation,beside if it has
          disadvantage,people won't bother
          buying them,it is even better than a
          bicycle, bicycle takes more effort to
          peddle, but car,just a gear push,you
          move...

The class cheers

                    ARIN
          a car carries more load,but a bicycle
          can't,and a bicycle...

The class cheering

                    HAKEEM
              (interrupt)
          Shut up!!!!

The class is silent and calm

     42.

Focus on hakeem gallivanting at the back of the classroom

                    HAKEEM
          Is it that you don't understand
          simple English,I said state the
          disadvantage of vehicle,and you come
          here stating rubbish between a car
          and a bicycle.....

                    ADDO (O.S)
               (Interrupt)
          well,she is right, isn't she?

Hakeem turns to see addo standing in front of the class

                    HAKEEM
          hey,Mr Man,what are you doing here,do
          you realize,this is a classroom!

                    ADDO
          oh, really,I don't think so, actually
          a class is suppose to be an
          interactive section,where student and
          teacher share ideas,where student are
          allow to express their opinion,not
          some kind of place where teacher
          force word and idea into
          students,beside she is right,a
          vehicle is better than bicycle!

The class cheers

                    ADDO
          You can't change the fact, because
          you can't afford one, doesn't mean
          you should condemn it,how can you
          condemn what you don't have idea or
          experience about,have you driven a
          car before or let me say can you
          drive at all,rather than condemning
          you should work and pray hard so you
          can afford one,and enjoy it's
          privilege,so you can stop peddling
          and stressing out your leg,oh look at
          leg, already developing muscle
          bump!!!!

The class laughing hard

                    HAKEEM
               (pissed off)
          get out!!!!

                    43.

                              ADDO
                    Sorry,I am going

Addo walk out of the class

The class still laughing heavily

                              HAKEEM
                    shut up!!!!

The class is silence

                              HAKEEM
                    you all have the gut to laugh at a
                    silly joke on me!!!,stand up all of
                    you!!

The class stand up,

we see addo driving off in his van

                              HAKEEM
                         (frustrated)
                    infact,this class is over!!!

Hakeem dash off aggressively

The class continue laughing and chattering heavily,
preparing to leave the class

                                             CUT TO:

EXT.SCHOOL.CONTINUOUS

we focus Hakeem walking out from the class aggressively to
his bicycle,

The student walking out of the class chattering,one after
the other

Hakeem aggressively take out his bicycle,hop on it,

About peddling,the bicycle collapse, landing hakeeem to the
ground,

We see Hakeem groans loudly in pain, holding his legs

We focus on some of the student laughing at him,

Some of the student walk to him, sympathizing

Focus on a student checking his bicycle wheel to see a stick
hook to the wheel,

She picks it up,to show Hakeem

Hakeem Groans loudly

The students help Hakeem up,Hakeem leaping and groaning as
they help him out of the school premises

Other student follows suit laughing

                                                    CUT TO:

EXT.HAKEEM'S HOUSE.EVENING

we focus on the student helping leaping hakeem to the
verandah

They help him sit on the bench,

One of them inspects his Hakeem leg

                    STUDENT
          it is broken,I think we need to call
          a nurse,

                    HAKEEM
          no,it is fine,it's fine,it is just a
          minor accident

                    STUDENT
          Are you sure sir,

                    HAKEEM
          yes,it is fine,I think it is late
          now,your parent will be worried,so
          you all should go home now,ok

we focus on the student leaving the scene, whispering to
each

We turn to Hakeem still sitting, soothing his leg, groaning
in pain

He stands up and leaps inside

                                                    CUT TO:

EXT.HAKEEM'S HOUSE.CONTINUOUS

We focus on a radio,

SELENSE BY CAVEMEN PLAYING

we focus on Hakeem backing the screen,shaking rhythmically
to the song,painting a potrait,

He standing on one leg,his broken leg hanging on a bench,

Soon he stop painting, dancing joyously

We focus on a female feet,walk in,

Hakeem still dancing,backing and ignorant of the person,
continue painting

We open on the overview of person ,it is Monalisa, carrying
a first aid box, standing behind Hakeem

She stare at Hakeem for a moment,coughs slightly to draw
attention

Hakeem stops dancing and turn back to glance at Monalisa

                    HAKEEM
          (hiss,ignore Monalisa, continues
          painting)
      It is just an imagination,

He paint for a moment and pause,

He turn back curiously again

                    HAKEEM
      wait,is this real,it is real right,

Close up on Monalisa face

                                        CUT TO:

EXT.HAKEEM'S HOUSE.CONTINUOUS

Still in the verandah

we see Monalisa dressing Hakeem who sitting on the bench
legs with bandage,

Hakeem   seem shy, watch on helplessly

                    MONALISA
          This is a very serious injury,you
          should be thankful to your
          student,who inform me about it,be
          careful,next time, bicycles can be
          extremely dangerous,you know

Hakeem still silent, watching on

Monalisa finish dressing the leg

                    MONALISA
                 (Stand up)
          so,I am done here, nothing much to be
          worried about,but if you notice any
          effect,you can check out the
          missionary health center ok

Hakeem nods childishly

Monalisa turns to leave

                    HAKEEM
          how much for it?

                    MONALISA
          you said?

Hakeem swallows his spit

                    HAKEEM
                 (retarded speech)
          I said,how much for the treatment?

                    MONALISA
                 (Smiles)
          actually,I work for the missionary,so
          our treatment are absolutely free,

Monalisa smiles and walk away

Close up on hakeem face,mouth agape watching Monalisa

                                        CUT TO:

INT.HAKEEM.DAY

Hakeem lying on the bed,

A close up on his face,

He smiling in fantasy

We zoom in,on his face

                                        FADE TO:

HAKEEM FANTASY SEQUENCE BEGINS

EXT.HAKEEM ROOM.DAY

we close up on Monalisa and Hakeem sitting on the bed
abouting kissing each other

still on the close up

                    47.

                    ADDO(V.O)
              Hakeem!!,Hakeem!!!!

HAKEEM FANTASY SEQUENCE ENDS

                                                    CUT TO:

INT.HAKEEM ROOM.CONTINUOUS

Focus on Hakeem still lying on the bed smiling

Addo standing,taps him

                    ADDO
              (calls out)
              Hakeem!!!

Hakeem regain consciousness,

Hakeem observe around in curiosity

                    ADDO
              what is wrong with you,I have been
              standing here,calling you!

                    HAKEEM
              (glancing around curiously)
              Did you see her?

                    ADDO
              (curious)
              see who?

Hakeem stand up, observing around

                    HAKEEM
              The girl!

                    ADDO
              (curious)
              what girl?

                    HAKEEM
              (Point to the Monalisa potrait on
              the wall)
              She,of course,she was here!

                    ADDO
              Hakeem,you have started again
                    HAKEEM
              I know what I am saying,she
              was here,she was the one who even
              bandage my leg,she told me she works
              with the missionary,

          48.

                    ADDO
               (Yells)
          Ah!!!!

                    HAKEEM
          what is wrong?

                    ADDO
          look,Hakeem,I am very sorry,I
          shouldn't have done it?

                    HAKEEM
          what are you saying?

                    ADDO
          I shouldn't have add stick to your
          bicycle wheel,if I had known that the
          accident will affect your
          psychology,look at what I have done
          to your brain now

Hakeem hiss

                    HAKEEM
          What is this one saying,I am sure of
          what I saw,you telling me I have a
          psychological issue

Hakeem walk toward the door

                    ADDO
          where are you going?

                    HAKEEM
          to search for her!

Hakeem walk out of the room to the exterior

                    ADDO
               (Hurries after Hakeem)
          Hakeem wait, don't run into the
          market,wait,oh God!

                                             CUT TO:

          EXT.MISSIONARY CENTER.EVENING

close up on Hakeem and addo in the van

                    ADDO
          are you sure of what you saw?

                    49.

                    HAKEEM
          I am serious,she talk to me,at first
          I doubted,but it was real!

                    ADDO
          Ok,if we discover she is not real,you
          will need to see a psychologist

Hakeem sighs

Both of them about alighting from the car

                                             CUT TO:

EXT.SISTER DORCAS OFFICE.MISSIONARY HEALTH CENTER.DAY

we see addo and Hakeem sitting in front of sister Dorcas

sister Dorcas stare at them curiosity for a moment

                    SISTER DORCAS
                 (Break the silence)
          so,what can I do for you?

Hakeem and addo hesitate

Sister Dorcas sight Hakeem bandage leg

                    SISTER DORCAS
          oh,your leg,does it need check up

Hakeem and addo nods sideway childishly

                    ADDO
                 (whisper to Hakeem)
          ask her

                    HAKEEM
                 (Whisper back to addo)
          you ask her!

                    ADDO
                 (whisper to Hakeem)
          I should....

Addo gives addo a sign look

Hakeem give him a stern look back,

Addo cough slightly

                    ADDO
          Ma'am, actually,I am,uhm,we are
          looking for a lady,slim, not too
          tall, actually she said,she work here
          as a nurse,

                    SISTER DORCAS
          do you need anything serious

                    ADDO
          no,not really we just want to confirm
          something

Sister Dorcas stare at them sternly for a moment

                    SISTER DORCAS
               (break the silence)
          actually,the lady you described,
          doesn't work here and have never been
          seen around here,

Close up on hakeem and addo face in disappointment

                    HAKEEM
          actually,she told me herself that she
          works here,

                    SISTER DORCAS
          like I said,she doesn't work here I
          work here alone,if you need any
          health related problem,I can help you
          with that

                    HAKEEM
          no,ma!,no health problem!

Close up on Hakeem in disappointment,

                                        CUT TO:

EXT.ROAD.DAY

A high angle shot to show an overview of addo van on the
lonely dusty road

                    ADDO(O.S)
          you see,she is not real,I think it is
          time you get your life together and
          stop chasing fantasies

Close up on Hakeem and addo in the van

                    HAKEEM
          i am so sure of what I saw

                         ADDO
              But you hear the sister,the girl
              doesn't work there,there is only one
              missionary in the community,if she is
              not there as she claims,she is
              obviously nowhere,if you continue
              like this,you might loose it,it just
              an advice,get your life together,if
              it seems overwhelming then see a good
              psychologist

we focus on Hakeem bows his head down in despair,

Addo igniting the van

                    CUT TO:

INT.CLASSROOM.DAY,

SCENE WITH MUTE AUDIO

we see Hakeem engaging his student in interactive lecture

Soon,we focus from Hakeem POV,Monalisa at the end of the
class, smiling at him

Close up on hakeem,close his eyes tightly, open it again,

Monalisa is nowhere to be found

He continues teaching

                    CUT TO:

INT.HAKEEM ROOM.DAY

we see Hakeem walk in, aggressively, tearing down all
Monalisa potrait on the wall

He destroys his drawing board furiously

Groaning in anger, he kneel down,bow his head and sobbing

                    CUT TO:
              EXT.FARM.DAY

Overview of the maiden working in the farm

we drift to see one of the soldier1,hands his guns to the
other soldier2,

The soldier1 walk to one of the maiden working in the farm,

He taps her and try to whisk her away

Other girl stops working, preventing soldier1

We cut to soldier2, ignorant and far off from the maiden
and soldier1

 he is behind a tree easing himself,litting a cigarette

We cut back to one of the maiden hacking soldier1 to death,

The maiden walk away from the site

We cut to soldier2 now sitting behind the tree smoking
heavily,

We see the maiden creeping behind from behind toward
soldier2,

One of the girl hit him hard on the head,

He falls to the ground, groaning heavily,

We focus on the maiden running off,

We cut back to soldier2 groaning in pain on the ground

                                              CUT TO:

EXT.GENERAL BASSEY'S BASE.NIGHT

A high angle shot to show the four maidens kneeling before
general bassey,captain Macaulay,soldier2 whose head is
bandage,and soldier3,

Focus on general bassey

                    GENERAL BASSEY
              you, girl really think,you can take
              down my soldier and get away with it,
              (sarcastically),wow so brave of
              you,so brave of you to have think of
              that,like where were you all running
              to,I run this whole province, don't
              you know that!,there is no hiding
              place,well I like your spirit,and
              obviously,such kind of spirit will be
              needed in the land of the dead,where
              you exactly belong

We focus on the maiden crying, pleading

INT.GENERAL BASE.ROOM.NIGHT

We see Monalisa,opens the window and glancing outside,

She fright,and rush out of the room.

                                              CUT TO:

EXT.GENERAL BASSEY'S BASE.CONTINUOUS

Everyone still in their position

                    GENERAL BASSEY
          you must have known,I don't take loss
          lightly,and so,an eye for eye (take
          out a pistol),and a tooth for a
          tooth, you all killed a soldier and
          so,you all....

General bassey shoot the first maiden

The wailing of the maiden increases

                    GENERAL BASSEY
                (point gun to the second maiden)
          will be killed....

General bassey shoot the second maiden

                    GENERAL BASSEY
                (Point to the third maiden)
          When you meet your family,tell them I
          am sorry for everything!

General bassey shoot the third girl

                    GENERAL BASSEY
                (point to the fourth maiden)
          And then....

                    MONALISA(O.S)
                (Interrupt)
          Stop,you bastard!!!

General bassey still holding the gun to the girl face,Turn
to see Monalisa,behind him

                    MONALISA
                (walk to the front of the fourth
                maiden, blocking her from general
                bassey gun)
          Haven't you tasted enough
          blood,bloodsucker!

                    GENERAL BASSEY
                 (still pointing the gun)
             get off her!!

                      MONALISA
              No!, I am not going anywhere,if you
              must kill her,you will kill me first,

General bassey fuming anger watches on as Monalisa picks the
fourth maiden up and whisk her inside the house

General bassey withdraw his gun,and groan in anger,

                                                   CUT TO:

EXT.RIVERSIDE.NIGHT

we focus Hakeem standing, watching as flame erupt the
portrait of Monalisa and drawing board infront of him

He watch sternly, sweating fuming,

We hear thunderstorms and heavy wind blowing

                                                   CUT TO:

EXT.GENERAL BASSEY'S BASE.NIGHT

we focus on the overview of the storey building

It is raining heavily accompany with thunderstorms

soldier2 and soldier3 taking shade at the verandah

We hear Monalisa wailing noise

                      GENERAL BASSEY(O.S)
                    (Fierce tone)
                 how many times have I told you not to
                 interfere in my military business,you
                 only duty is to be a wife....

IN THE ROOM-

we transition to see general brutalizing and whipping
Monalisa with his belt

Monalisa wailing, trying to avoid the whip,

soon she manage to escape general bassey,run off the room,

General bassey run after her

                                                   CUT TO:

EXT.GENERAL BASSEY'S BASE.CONTINUOUS

Still raining heavily

we focus the overview of the building,the soldiers still the
verandah

we see Monalisa crying, running out of house, away from
compound

The two soldier about chasing after

 general bassey rush out of the house and stop in the
verandah

                         GENERAL BASSEY
                       (To the soldiers)
              Leave her alone,she won't go far,

The soldier stops

They all watch as Monalisa goes out of sight

thunderstorm and raining continue

                                                  CUT TO:

EXT.RIVERSIDE.CONTINUOUS

we focus on Hakeem holding onto his bicycle in the rain,
watches the firespot,which is already quench by the raining

He watch for moment,then turn and leaves, pushing his
bicycle

                                                  CUT TO:

EXT.ROAD.NIGHT

we focus Monalisa sitting on a stone by the roadside, in the
rain, sobbing

Soon we focus on Hakeem pushing his bicycle in the rain,in
despair

he sight Monalisa, ignores her, continue pushing his bicycle

                         HAKEEM
                    (mutters to himself)
                 she is not real?

Hakeem still pushing his bicycle,stops for moment,turns back
to glance at Monalisa

Close up on hakeem,he take a breath,close his eye tightly,
glance at Monalisa,

We close up on Monalisa,still sitting sobbing,

Hakeem now in front of her, holding onto his bicycle

                    HAKEEM
               (Curious)
          who exactly,are you?

Monalisa ignores Hakeem, still sobbing,

Hakeem observes her for a moment to see bruise on her

Close on hakeem sighing

                                        CUT TO:

INT.HAKEEM'S HOUSE.ROOM.NIGHT

We close up Monalisa sitting on the bed,

We see Hakeem hand, stretching a cup to her

                    MONALISA
               (glance at hakeem,takes the cup)
          thank you!!

We cut to addo walking in from the exterior,

he shocks on seeing Monalisa

He hurriedly walk to Hakeem,drag him to the corner

                    ADDO
               (Whisper to Hakeem nervously)
          Am I going psycho?

                    HAKEEM
               (Curious)
          psycho?

                    ADDO
          it seems like I can see your fantasy
          now,can you see the lady on the bed?

Hakeem smiles mockingly

                    HAKEEM
          actually,it is exactly what you see

                    ADDO
          you can see her too,right?

                    HAKEEM
          of,course I can,I told you she is
          real!

We cut to Monalisa still sitting on the bed, observing round

Addo still nervous walk slowly to her

                    ADDO
               (to Monalisa)
          Hello

Monalisa smiles to addo

                    MONALISA
               (Wave slightly)
          hello!!

Monalisa continues observing around

Addo still staring at her curiously,scratch his head

                    HAKEEM
               (To Monalisa)
          I know you will be farmish,I think I
          will go prepare something for you,

Monalisa smiles at Hakeem

Hakeem walk to the interior,

Addo follow him, immediately

IN THE KITCHEN

we see Hakeem arrange kitchen utensil,

Addo enters

                    ADDO
          what are you trying to do?

                    HAKEEM
          What does it look like I am doing,
          trying to cook, of course,

Addo laughs mockingly

                    ADDO
          so, because you have seen a woman,you
          suddenly develop culinary skill,or
          have you forgotten,you can't cook,you
          want to serve a guest blunder

Addo start laughing again

Hakeem stare at addo disgustingly,in confusion state

IN THE ROOM

Monalisa sitting on the bed,playing with her fingers

Hakeem walk in from the kitchen

He Smiles at her and walk out

                                        CUT TO:

INT.KITCHEN.HAKEEM'S HOUSE.CONTINUOUS

SCENE WITHOUT AUDIO,JUST MUSIC

we see Hakeem and addo dressed in appron, engaging cooking
and funny activities

                                        CUT TO:

INT.ROOM.HAKEEM'S HOUSE.CONTINUOUS

we focus Monalisa sitting on the bed

a plate of food on the table before her,

Monalisa glance up to see Addo and Hakeem standing front of
her, Watching at her nervously

Both men still dressed in appron

Monalisa takes a taste from the food in expectancy

She nods in acceptance,

She smiles at them,

They smiles at her back childishly

She continues eating

Hakeem gives addo a blink,

Addo smiles back

                                        CUT TO:

we cut to see Addo packing the plate,

While Hakeem cleaning the table, mistakenly spill water from the cup on Monalisa,

Addo return to see hakeem action

He picks up a rag immediately and starting clean water from Monalisa dress

Monalisa take the rag and cleaning it herself,

We see Hakeem demonstrating in apology,

He picks the cup and walk away

IN THE KITCHEN

we see Hakeem drops the cup,and hugs addo passionately and joyously,

Addo struggling to free himself from Hakeem grips

FADE OUT:

INT.ROOM.HAKEEM'S HOUSE.MORNING

we fade in to see Monalisa waking up from a sleep

Still focus on Monalisa,who is curious,addo and Hakeem snoring heavily

She glances down the bed to see Addo and Hakeem lying asleep,recklessly on the ground

She get off the bed, avoiding body touch with Hakeem and addo, who are still sleeping

CUT TO:

INT.HAKEEM'S HOUSE.ROOM.CONTINUOUS

we focus on Monalisa backing the screen, admiring the art portrait on the wall

We cut to show her face,

We see Hakeem standing beside her,drowsy and sleepy

She turns to glance at Hakeem then turn back to the art potrait

                    MONALISA
          this art are beautiful,it has
          something striking,that touch the
          soul,it communicate,I can tell it's
          from a great artist with good
          fantasy.....

Hakeem still sleepy,sight the time on the clock,9:20am

                    HAKEEM
                (nervous)
          Jesus Christ!!

Monalisa in curiousity turn to see Hakeem gallivanting in
confusion,

Hakeem eventually pick up his toothbrush from the container
on the desk and dash out of the room to the exterior

We focus on Monalisa face in curiosity

Hakeem enters again,his face wet, hurriedly,drop the
toothbrush in the container and walk to pick the bucket at
the corner

                    MONALISA
                (Curious)
          What is wrong?

                    HAKEEM
                (searching around)
          I have a class to attend to?

                    MONALISA
          are you a student?

                    HAKEEM
                (Sight a tower at the edge,walk to
                it)
          I am a teacher,my student are waiting
          for me, oh my God I am late again

                    MONALISA
          But,it is Saturday, there are no
          School on Saturday?

                    HAKEEM
                (Bend to pick the tower)
          Is it?

Hakeem curious to check the calendar on the wall,

He sighs in relief

                    HAKEEM
          It is skip me

Hakeem walk to the corner and drop the bucket

Hakeem toss the tower to the ground

Close up on the tower covering addo face,who is still fast
asleep on the ground

EXT.HAKEEM'S HOUSE.CONTINUOUS

we focus on Hakeem and Monalisa sitting on the bench in the
verandah

Hakeem avoiding eye contact with Monalisa

                    MONALISA
          so,you are an artist and a teacher,so
          tell me what else do you do?

                    HAKEEM
          Poem!

                    MONALISA
          Are you kidding me?

                    HAKEEM
          No,I am poet,but mainly for fun,

                    MONALISA
          You are true definition of an Art
          God,look at you,embroided with
          talent,do you know what I have
          meaning to have beautiful potrait of
          myself,I am core lover of art, i
          don't know if you can do that for me
          please

Hakeem sighs

                    HAKEEM
          well, I can,but only at where I draw
          my inspiration from

                    MONALISA
          And where is it?

                    HAKEEM
          the Riverside

                    MONALISA
          then what are we waiting for?,let go

Monalisa stands up, waiting for Hakeem to stand

                                            CUT TO:

EXT.ROAD.DAY

An overview of Monalisa holding onto Hakeem and his drawing
equipment as he peddles the bicycle

                                            CUT TO:

EXT.RIVERSIDE.DAY

We focus on the radio playing

COOL JAZZ PIANO MUSIC PLAYING

We focus on Monalisa sitting on the chair,posing, smiling in
front of the riverside

We drift back to focus Hakeem standing,drawing a potrait of
her

                                            CUT TO:

EXT.RIVERSIDE.CONTINUOUS

we focus Monalisa and Hakeem sitting by the riverbank

Monalisa admiring the portrait

Hakeem head down, playing with his fingers

                    MONALISA
          this is really beautiful,I didn't
          believe they are amazing artist in
          this potrait,the two art I love
          much,are poem and painting,sadly I
          don't have talent in any of the
          two,and here the both
          talent,embroided in person,

Hakeem still playing with his fingers smiles

                    HAKEEM
          well,it takes a good inspiration and
          determination,then you can do
          anything, although talent are born
          with some persons,but other persons
          can develop it as well,just the right
          inspiration needed

                    MONALISA
          you think,I can compose a poem and
          paint an art

                    HAKEEM
          if you wish to,

                    MONALISA
          ok,boss!

Monalisa stands up,drops the portrait on the ground,walk
into the river playfully

                    MONALISA
               (demonstrating)
          first,I need inspiration from the
          river,

She playfully close her eyes and takes a deep breath

She open her eye,clear her throat,stares at Hakeem

                    MONALISA
          I can hear the bird singing a song of
          melodious,the tree clapping in
          accolade,as the river flows,
          spreading the good vibe along.

we focus Hakeem smiling

                    MONALISA
          How was it?

                    HAKEEM
               (Still smiling)
          perfect!!

                    MONALISA
          really?

Hakeem nods

                    MONALISA
               (walking out of the river toward
               hakeem)
          Now,your turn

                    HAKEEM
               (Nervous)
          What?

                    MONALISA
          Let's hear your poem, monsieur!

Hakeem hesitate

                    HAKEEM
          I am not in the mood

                    MONALISA
          come on,let hear it

Monalisa dragging Hakeem hand up,making him to stand,

                    MONALISA
               (walking backward toward the river)
          Now to the river for inspiration

Monalisa still walking backward,trip

Falling to the ground,Hakeem grab her

They lock eyes for a moment,

Close up on them still in the position

Monalisa regain consciousness and free herself from Hakeem
grips,walk away

Hakeem scratch his head in confusion

                                        CUT TO:

EXT.RIVERSIDE.EVENING

we see Hakeem and Monalisa sitting on the ground by the
riverbank

Monalisa tossing stone to the river

                    MONALISA
          you see,it has been a long time,I
          experience this kind of freedom,
          going outside the wall, visiting
          riverside,good old memories

                    HAKEEM
          why?, don't you go out

                    MONALISA
          Well,there are some little
          privilege,some people don't enjoy,so
          tell me about yourself and your
          brother

                    HAKEEM
               (curious)
          My brother?

                    MONALISA
          yes,addo!

Hakeem laugh

                    HAKEEM
          addo is not brother,just a buddy,we
          grew up together, share a lot
          together, although we argue alot

                    MONALISA
          Argue?,what do you guys argue about?

                    HAKEEM
          So many things,imagine,him telling a
          vehicle is better than a bicycle

                    MONALISA
               (Laughing)
          really,you guys argue about that?

                    HAKEEM
          yes,is it a crime to?

                    MONALISA
               (still laughing)
          No,not at all,I thought those kind of
          arguement are meant for kids..

Monalisa glance at Hakeem

                    MONALISA
          I am sorry, don't mean to upset you
          but....

Monalisa burst into laughter

Hakeem stare at her in engrossment

Monalisa still laughing,notice Hakeem

She stops laughing,and sighs

Hakeem still staring

                    MONALISA
               (stands up)
          It is late already,I think we should
          be going

Hakeem regain consciousness and stands up

                                        CUT TO:

EXT.GENERAL BASSEY'S OFFICE.DAY

We focus on general bassey,in thought, tapping his finger to
the table

We now focus on captain macaulay watching him

                    CAPTAIN MACAULAY
                 (Break the silence)
            I think she is not coming back

                    GENERAL BASSEY
                 (Nervous tone)
            No,no,it can't happen, she have to
            come back,she can go anywhere,you and
            your men go search for her now,every
            nook and cranny,it must come back
            here

we see captain Macaulay salute general bassey and walk away

Close up on general bassey fuming nervously

                                              CUT TO:

EXT.ROAD.DAY

NO AUDIO,STRING MUSIC

we see captain soldier and soldier2 showing pedestrian,a
pics of Monalisa, asking for description,

Pedestrian nods negatively

We cut to see an overview of addo van being stop by captain
Macaulay

we see captain macaulay showing the picture of Monalisa

Addo in Surprise,takes the picture from captain Macaulay and
glance at it sternly,.

He give captain Macaulay the picture and nod negatively

Captain Macualay walk away,

Addo drives off

                                              CUT TO:

INT.HAKEEM'S HOUSE.ROOM.MORNING

we focus on Monalisa holding a paper,reading it content to
Hakeem who is sitting on the bed

                    MONALISA
               (reading)
          How long can i continuing being slave
          to myself,how long can I keep leaving
          in the shadow of myself,being afraid
          to take the next step,oh, probably
          not the fear though, because the last
          step I took,mess me up,now I am here,
          stuck again,not again,the next step
          is oblivious and might end the
          unknown.....

                                                  CUT TO:

EXT.HAKEEM'S HOUSE.CONTINUOUS

we focus on addo van coming to a stop

we see addo alighting and rushing into the house

                                                  CUT TO:

INT.HAKEEM'S HOUSE.ROOM.CONTINUOUS

we focus on Monalisa still reading the poem

                    MONALISA
          my fear is just an emotion,not
          real,but what if they give birth to
          my reality and I......

Addo enter nervously and whisk Hakeem outside immediately

We focus on Monalisa stop reading,watching curiously

                                                  CUT TO:

EXT.HAKEEM'S HOUSE.CONTINUOUS

we see addo dragging Hakeem outside from the house

                    HAKEEM
               (curious)
          what is wrong?

                    ADDO
               (whispering to Hakeem)
          Military men are looking for her

                68.

                    HAKEEM
                 (curious)
          For who?

                    ADDO
                 (point inside)
          she,of course!

We see the troops van drives in roughly,

Captain Macaulay and soldier2 and a KID alight,

The kid points to addo and Hakeem immediately

At the same time we see Monalisa walk out of the house,
curiously

Soldier2 walk to Monalisa whisking her to the van

We see Monalisa protesting,

We focus on captain macaulay walk closely to addo and stare
at him in the eye furiously

Close up on Addo in panic, swallows his saliva

Captain Macaulay walk away to the van and they drives off

We see addo sighs in relief,

Hakeem watching the van helplessly

                                                  CUT TO:

INT.HAKEEM'S HOUSE.ROOM.CONTINUOUS

we see Hakeem sitting on the bed, in despair

                    ADDO
                 (gallivanting nervously)
          so, she is a daughter of the great
          general bassey,no wonder no one knows
          much about her,he must be so
          overprotective of her,I think you
          should just back off her,it is very
          dangerous...

Hakeem sight Monalisa potrait,

He stands up immediately,walk to pick the portrait,

                    ADDO
          Hakeem, where do you think you are
          going?

Hakeem ignores and walk out of the house

                                        CUT TO:

EXT.HAKEEM'S HOUSE.CONTINUOUS

We see addo rushing out of the house to see Hakeem holding
the potrait riding out in his bicycle

                                        CUT TO:

EXT.GENERAL BASSEY'S BASE.DAY

we focus on the fourth maiden sweeping the compound,

We see the captain Macaulay,soldier2 alight from the van,

Captain Macaulay take out Monalisa from the van,

We focus on the fourth maiden stops sweeping, watching
captain Macaulay whisking Monalisa inside the house

The ladies lock eyes

                                        CUT TO:

INT.ROOM.GENERAL BASSEY'S BASE.CONTINUOUS

we focus on Monalisa sitting on the bed,head down in thought

General bassey standing in front of her

                    GENERAL BASSEY
                 (innocently)
            is that bad that you have to run away
            from me,

general bassey bend over to Monalisa

                    GENERAL BASSEY
            I know I messed up and hurt you
            bitterly,but I don't want to loose
            you,you are my everything,my
            happiness,my gold, look I have turn a
            new leaf ok,I won't do anything to
            hurt you anymore,

Monalisa glance at general bassey

General bassey sit beside Monalisa

                    GENERAL BASSEY
          I promise, Can't you see,I didn't
          kill the girl again,she is alive,I am
          a change person,I won't do anything
          to hurt you again,just don't leave me
          again,I can't stand thought of losing
          you!

Monalisa start sobbing,

General hugs her passionately

                    GENERAL BASSEY
          it is ok, everything is fine now

close up on both of them still in the position

                                        CUT TO:

EXT.GENERAL BASSEY'S BASE.CONTINUOUS

we see Hakeem,holding the potrait rides in,to see the fourth
maiden still sweeping,

She stare at him,in curiousity, sweeping

We see hakeem inspecting his bicycle

At the same time soldier2 walk out of the house

                    SOLDIER2
          hey,Mr Man what are you doing here!!

Hakeem stands up,nervous

Soon General bassey and captain Macaulay walk out

                    GENERAL BASSEY
          Who is that?

Hakeem still nervous

                    HAKEEM
               (counting word)
          Uhmm,I am an artist,I bring Monalisa
          potrait

General bassey takes the portrait from hakeem ,he glances at
it and smiles

 Hakeem enters his bicycle immediately and rides out,

Close up on general bassey stare sternly at Hakeem as he
rides on

                71.

                                              CUT TO:

INT.GENERAL BASE.ROOM.CONTINUOUS

Close up on Monalisa sitting on the bed

we see general bassey enters,gives the portrait to her

                    GENERAL BASSEY
          I think this belongs to you

Monalisa takes the potrait,nervously, admiring it

 General bassey turns to leave

                    MONALISA
               (Nervously)
          did you....

                    GENERAL BASSEY
               (Turn to Monalisa)
          Don't be scared,he is just an
          artist,I don't have business with
          him,like I said I am a change person

General bassey walk away,

Focus on Monalisa admiring the portrait

                                              CUT TO:

EXT.HAKEEM'S HOUSE.CONTINUOUS

we see addo sittitng by the verandah, nervous

We see Hakeem rides in,in his bicycle

Addo stand up immediately,walk to him

                    ADDO
               where did you go?

                    HAKEEM
          to Monalisa,to give her the portrait

                    ADDO
          do you realize the danger of what you
          are doing?, general bassey is way a
          dangerous man to Toy with it

                    HAKEEM
          it is just a potrait I return,nothing
          much

                    ADDO
          I know your real intention with
          Monalisa,that why I am cautioning
          before it escalate to something you
          can't run from,you heard stories of
          the general,so you better stop now!!

                    HAKEEM
               (walking out on addo)
          You worry too much

Hakeem enters the house

Addo sighs and enter the house

                                        CUT TO:

EXT.GENERAL BASSEY'S BASE.ROOM.MORNING

we focus on Monalisa dresses up in nurse attire in staring
at the mirror,inspecting herself

She walk away from the mirror and pick up her bag from the
bed and walk out of the room

                                        CUT TO:

EXT.GENERAL BASSEY'S BASE.MORNING

we focus on the fourth maiden sweeping,

While soldier3 standing by the Mercedes Benz

We see Monalisa walk out of the house,head to the car,

soldier3 prevents her from entering the car

                    MONALISA
          what are you doing?

                    SOLDIER3
          an order from the general says,you
          can't leave the premises

                    MONALISA
          do you realize,I am going to the
          health center

                    SOLDIER3
          health center, inclusively

Monalisa pause,in thought, looking pissed off,

She sighs and walk inside aggressively,

We focus on the fourth maiden still sweeping

                                        CUT TO:

INT.SISTER DORCAS OFFICE.MISSIONARY HEALTH CENTER.DAY

SCENE WITHOUT AUDIO JUST STRING MUSIC

we see sister Dorcas gallivanting about,

She glances at the clock,Then pick up her rosary and walk
out of the office

                        CUT TO:

INT.HALL.MISSIONARY HEALTH CENTER.DAY

SCENE WITHOUT AUDIO,JUST STRING MUSIC

we see sister Dorcas addressing the elderly people

                                CUT TO:

INT.ROOM.GENERAL BASSEY'S BASE.CONTINUOUS

we see Monalisa sitting in front of the desk, writing,

We see the fourth maiden walk in,

Serving Monalisa desk with tea and bread

                    MONALISA
          thank you!!

Fourth maiden about walking off

                    MONALISA
               (still writing)
          hello, come,

Fourth maiden walk in,stand in front of Monalisa

                    MONALISA
               (Glance at her)
          sit

Fourth maiden sit on the bed

Monalisa abandon her writing

                    MONALISA
          So I don't know your name

                    FOURTH MAIDEN
               (Nervous)
          Habeeb!

          We see monalisa observing habeeb,who
          playing with her finger

                    MONALISA
          Habeeb,can I talk with you

Habeeb nods slightly

                    MONALISA
          habeeb,I know you are going a lot
          right due to the general action,and a
          lot going through,but you see I am
          different,I am going through the same
          pain as you,I was also abducted like
          you,my village was raided,my parent
          killed,I am just like you, just that
          I enjoy more privilege, because of
          the general interest in me,but I
          don't fancy that,I want real freedom
          just like you,why I am saying this is
          because I want us to be friends more
          than a slave and a master,you are not
          my slave,hope you understand

Habeeb nods

Monalisa smiles, spread her arm,

They hugs

                    MONALISA
               (turn to the desk)
          you see,I am trying to compose a
          poem,I don't know if you can help out

Habeeb glance at the paper,Monalisa is writing

                                        CUT TO:

INT.ROOM.GENERAL BASSEY'S BASE.CONTINUOUS

SCENE WITHOUT AUDIO,JUST STRING

we see habeeb joyously talking,demonstrating as Monalisa
laughs on and write,

                                        CUT TO:

EXT.GENERAL BASSEY'S BASE.CONTINUOUS

SCENE WITHOUT AUDIO,JUST STRING MUSIC

we see sister Dorcas in discussion with soldier3

Soldier3 direct her inside

Sister Dorcas smile and enter the house

                              CUT TO:
                    INT.ROOM.GENERA
                       L BASSEY'S
                    BASE.CONTINUOUS

We focus Monalisa and habeeb laughing

                    MONALISA
               (Glancing at the paper)
            This is perfect!!!

                    HABEEB
            yes,poem are expression of feelings!

Sister Dorcas walk in

                    MONALISA
               oh,sister Dorcas

Habeeb pick up the empty teacup and walk away

                              CUT TO:

INT.ROOM.GENERAL BASSEY'S BASE.CONTINUOUS

we focus on sister Dorcas and Monalisa sitting on the bed

                    SISTER DORCAS
            If,all this are happening,why don't
            we just report to the overall head
            general,I can do that you know

Monalisa chuckles

                    MONALISA
            you see,they are all the same,you
            think the head general is not aware
            of this action,they work hand in
            hand,so reporting general bassey is a
            just a futile effort,and would lead
            to more damage,there is nothing we
            can do,than just watch,oh gosh,I just
            want to be free from this shackles
            and torment,

Monalisa breaks down in despair

                    SISTER DORCAS
          come on,Monalisa don't be sad,there
          is always a way out,and that Jesus
          Christ, don't be despair,the good
          Lord knows all you are passing
          through,and I am sure you will come
          to your rescue one day,Christ is
          greater than all general on Earth

Monalisa sighs

                    MONALISA
          thank you,sister

                    SISTER DORCAS
          You are welcome,I think I have to get
          going,you know there is a lot to do
          at the missionary

Sister Dorcas stands up

                    MONALISA
          Eem,wait,can you help me deliver
          something to someone

Monalisa hands sister Dorcas an envelope

                    MONALISA
          the name and address are in written
          on it

Sister glance at the envelope,smiles and walk away

We focus on Monalisa lays on the bed in distress

                    CUT TO:

INT.CLASSROOM.DAY

we focus on Hakeem,gallivanting the calm classroom,reading a
book to the students

Hakeem sight sister Dorcas at the entrance of the classroom

We see Hakeem take permission from the student

He walk outside to meet sister Dorcas,

She hands an envelope to Hakeem and walk away

Hakeem stare at the envelope in curiousity

He shrugs and walk back to the classroom

 Hakeem continue reading the book

INT.ROOM.HAKEEM'S HOUSE.DAY

we see HAKEEM sitting on the bed, reading the letter from
sister dorcas

                    MONALISA (V.O)
          we only become a slave,when we can't
          overcome our fear,truly fear is an
          emotion and unreal,it become a
          reality, when we accept them,and make
          them god over us,w

          We see Hakeem smiling,he check the
          envelope,

We close up on the envelope to see an inscription "MONALISA"

                                              CUT TO:
          INT.ROOM.HAKEEM'S HOUSE.DAY

we focus on Hakeem sitting by the desk,writing

                    HAKEEM(v.o)
          how can I over fear,when it has a
          built a hefty wall around,oh yes,I
          try to break through......
                                              CUT TO:

INT.ROOM.HAKEEM'S HOUSE.DAY

we transition to see Monalisa laying on the bed, smiling and
reading a letter,

                    HAKEEM (V.O)
          I discover,it is made of steel,a
          strong metal,and I am not a
          blacksmith,neither do I know how to
          cut iron,I try scaling through,but it
          is too high for my reach,I am no
          jumper,and I don't want my heel
          broken

soon we see Monalisa sit up, laughing

   78.

Soon she glance at her potrait and glance at general
portrait

She sighs,and walk to her desk,take out a paper and start
writing

                    MONALISA (V.O)
                 (writing and reading out aloud)
            It is not a wall,rather a
            psychology,thought of the mind,and
            reality are more difficult than
            thought of mind, the writer,say if
            you get through thought of the mind
            you can get through the reality of
            life,but reality is a mighty soldier
            strong than the thought of the
            mind,so I think fear is just an
            emotion but reality is the real
            war....

we see Monalisa drops the pen,fall to distress thought

                                            CUT TO:

EXT.RIVERSIDE.DAY

we focus on Hakeem sitting by Riverside glancing through
monalisa's letter

He falls to thought for a moment

He picks out his pen and start write,

He pause for a moment and package the letter an envelope,he
takes out a tape from his radio and put it in the envelope

He stand up,pick up his radio and bicycle, walking away

                                            CUT TO:

INT.ROOM.HAKEEM'S HOUSE.DAY

we see addo walk in, gallivanting

he sight the letter on desk

He picks it and read through an inscription "FROM MONALISA"

Soon we see Hakeem walk in,drop the radio on the desk

                    ADDO
            what is all this letter

Hakeem take the letter from addo

                    ADDO
          This will get you and I killed,you
          should know that,why are you too
          stubborn to listen

                    HAKEEM
          Sorry,I don't think I want to
          stop,why are we even afraid,she is
          just a general daughter,beside the
          general won't marry her daughter

                    ADDO
          oh,you think the general will give
          his daughter to a low life like
          you,huh

                    HAKEEM
          oh,I am a low life,what about
          you,huh,you forgot I pick you up from
          the street oh,

                    ADDO
          you are going to insult me now,right,
          but let me tell you,you took me from
          the street,but over the years,I have
          achieve more than you,look at
          you,what do you have to your
          name,just a worn out bicycle and you
          think,you can get a general
          daughter,what a fool you are,let me
          ask,can you approach a lady in the
          face,you think, writing poem,will
          entice,you just a shrimp,

We see Hakeem fuming,at addo,

                    ADDO
          what do you want to do,huh,beat
          me,you are weakling and can't do
          anything,

Hakeem dash out of the room aggressively

 Addo sighs aggressively,sink to the bed

                                        CUT TO:

INT.ROOM.GENERAL BASSEY'S HOUSE.DAY

we focus Monalisa curiously opening an envelope, reading
through,

We focus on the paper, inscription. "PLEASE MEET ME AT THE RIVERSIDE,I HAVE SOMETHING TO TELL YOU,MEANWHILE ENJOY THE MUSIC"

we focus on Monalisa face in curiousity,

She take out the tape from the envelope

She put it on a radio on the desk

LET HER GO BY PASSENGER PLAYING

We focus on her laying in the bed, smiling

MONALISA FANTASY SEQUENCE BEGINS

EXT.RIVERSIDE.NIGHT

Music still playing

we see Monalisa and Hakeem sitting round a firespot by the riverbank

Hakeem holding a guitar playing
'

While Monalisa watch,

We cut to see them playing hide and seek

The music ends

                                                        CUT TO:

MONALISA FANTASY ENDS

INT.ROOM.GENERAL BASSEY'S BASE.CONTINUOUS

close up on Monalisa opens her to see general bassey reading Hakeem letter

She panics

                         GENERAL BASSEY
                    Where is this from?

Monalisa hesitate

                         GENERAL BASSEY
                    so,this is what you want huh

Monalisa still fright

General bassey dash out of the room aggressively

Monalisa groans in anger

                                        CUT TO:

EXT.RIVERSIDE.EVENING

We see Hakeem holding on to his bicycle,backing the screen,
watching the river, waiting patiently

We close up on him,to see him holding a flower

He toss the flower to the river,sigh heavily and walk away,
pushing the bicycle

                                        CUT TO:

EXT.RIVERSIDE.EVENING

An overview of general bassey mercedez benz halting in front
the river

General bassey, captain macaulay, soldier3 alight from the
car,

They glances around,enter the car and drive off

                        CUT TO;

EXT.HAKEEM'S HOUSE.EVENING

we focus general bassey car halting in the compound

we turn to see Addo walking out of the house in curiosity

General bassey and his boys alight from the car

We focus on addo nervous face

                    GENERAL BASSEY
                (Furious, pointing a gun)
              Where is Hakeem!!!

Addo nervous,pointing outside

                    GENERAL BASSEY
              can you talk,cat got your tongue?

                    ADDO
                (Nervous)
              he is not here,

                    GENERAL BASSEY
                         (Furious)
               I am asking,where he.....

A gunshot is heard

we close up on general bassey,in surprise,glancing at his
gun

We focus on addo dead in the ground,

General bassey staggering backward in shock,

He thens order his men to the car

The car drive off

We focus on addo corpse on the ground

                                              CUT TO:

INT.SITTING ROOM.GENERAL BASSEY BASE.EVENING

We transition to sister Dorcas corpse,from bullet shot,
laying reckless in the chair

                                              CUT TO:

EXT.GENERAL BASSEY'S BASE.EVENING

we focus on habeeb sweeping the compound,

We see Hakeem stopping the bicycle in the compound

Still holding on the bicycle

                    HAKEEM
                         (screaming)
               Monalisa!!,can you hear me,come out,I
               want to talk something important to
               you,

Habeeb stands watching

we see Monalisa rush out of the house, trying to whisk
Hakeem away

                    MONALISA
               You need to get out,
               immediately,please,he is after you?

                    HAKEEM
               I am not afraid of your father!

                        MONALISA
            he is not my father!,

                        HAKEEM
                    (Surprise)
            He is not your father?,then who is
            he?

Monalisa give him stern look

Hakeem still shock,mouth agape

                        MONALISA
            you have to go now

Hakeem perplex

We see the troops rides in,

Monalisa,nervous

                        MONALISA
                    (Nervous)
                go,now!!!!

We see Hakeem hurriedly riding out on his bicycle

Soldier3 immediately rush to him and grab him down

                        MONALISA
                    (cries out)
                Nooo!!!!

We close up,on soldier3 still holding Hakeem to the ground

We see general bassey walk to them,bring out a gun and point
to Hakeem

We focus on Monalisa,in fright,close her mouth with her palm
and close her eyes

Still focus on Monalisa,we hear a gun shot

Tears drop from Monalisa face,she opens her eye,

We focus on general bassey pointing gun up

                        GENERAL BASSEY
                    (To soldier3)
                Lock him up

we see the soldiers whisking Hakeem away

    84.

Focus on Monalisa sighs in relief,

General bassey walk pass her,glancing at her furiously

Captain Macaulay following general bassey,as they enters the house

                                                        CUT TO:

INT.GENERAL'S OFFICE.CONTINUOUS

we focus on general bassey sitting on his seat

                    CAPTAIN MACAULAY
              why didn't you do it sir?

                    GENERAL BASSEY
                  (curious)
              Do what?

                    CAPTAIN MACAULAY
              the man,why didn't you shoot him

  General bassey grins

                    GENERAL BASSEY
              you see, that type of death is too
              quick,when someone flaunt my order,I
              execute without second thought, but
              when someone toys with my gold,I
              enjoy watching them dying out
              slowly,so ,by sunset tomorrow I will
              sit with my queen and watch him burn
              alive in flame

General bassey laughs out wickedly

                                                        CUT TO:

EXT.GENERAL BASSEY'S BASE.EVENING

we focus on habeeb holding on to a broom, eavesdropping at window,

She walk away immediately

                                                        CUT TO:

INT.ROOM.GENERAL BASSEY'S BASE.EVENING

we focus on Monalisa laying on the bed in thought

The door squeak open

Monalisa turn to see habeeb

                    HABEEB
          they are going to burn him alive
          tomorrow

                    MONALISA
               (sit up)
          How did you know that?

                    HABEEB
          I overheard the general telling
          captain Macaulay,

                    MONALISA
          what are we going to do?

Habeeb sighs

                    HABEEB
          I think,I have a plan!

                    MONALISA
               (curious)
          what plan?

Close up on habeeb smiling

                                        CUT TO:
                                   EXT.GENERAL
                                     BASSEY'S
                                   BASE.NIGHT

we open on soldier2 and soldier3,sitting outside on a bench,
smoking playing card game

We see habeeb walking out from the house toward the soldier
carrying a tray of food,

She put on the bench and turn to leave

                    SOLDIER2
               (Suspiciously)
          Hey,come back here

Habeeb turn back,curiously

                    SOLDIER2
          take a taste from the food

Soldier3 glance at soldier2

we see the habeeb hesitate,

                    SOLDIER2
          are you deaf,

Habeeb smiles slightly and sighs

She open the tray and takes a taste,and walk away

The soldiers start eating

                                        CUT TO:

EXT.GENERAL BASSEY'S BASE.NIGHT

We focus on the edge of the building

No one in site

Soon we see habeeb walking in, convulsing and vomiting,till
she collapse to the ground dead

                                        CUT TO:

INT.ROOM.GENERAL BASSEY'S BASE.CONTINUOUS

we see Monalisa laying seductively on the bed

The door squeak open

General bassey enters and stare at Monalisa who is seducing
him for a moment

                    GENERAL BASSEY
          What are you up to?

                    MONALISA
               (Soothing general bassey)
          well, trying to say thank you,for
          keeping to your promise,of not
          hurting anyone again

                    GENERAL BASSEY
               (Romancing Monalisa)
          well,I kept to my promise,but that
          doesn't mean I will release him
          soon,I want him to learn a lesson,so
          he will be staying in the jail for
          quite a time,till I am satisfied

                    MONALISA

We see Monalisa push general bassey seductively to the bed,

She climbs on,brings out a knife slowly from her gown and
stab him dead, fiercely

Monalisa in panics,run off of the room.

                                            CUT TO:

EXT.GENERAL BASSEY'S BASE.CONTINUOUS

We see Monalisa creeping out of the house,to see the dead
body of the soldiers,laying recklessly on the ground beside
the bench with plate of unfinish food

She creeps to the corner of the house

we see Monalisa sight habeeb corpse on the ground

She close her mouth in tear,fall to her kneel down beside
it, wailing

Still crying,she holds to the corpse

                                            CUT TO:

INT.ROOM.GENERAL BASSEY'S BASE.CONTINUOUS

We focus on Hakeem in the dark empty room playing with his
finger,

The door opens,

we focus on Monalisa standing by the door

                    MONALISA
                 (Whispering)
            Come out!!!

Hakeem stands up immediately and follows Hakeem as they walk
out of the room

                                            CUT TO:

EXT.GENERAL BASSEY'S BASE.CONTINUOUS

we focus Monalisa and hakeem walking fast by edge of the
building

                        HAKEEM
          why didn't you tell me,you were
          married,

                        MONALISA
          I am not married!

                        HAKEEM
          then who is general bassey to you!!

we see both of them walking pass habeeb,

Monalisa unconcerned walking pass the corpse

                        HAKEEM
                   (nervous)
          oh,my God,this is a corpse,what is
          going

Soon we hear a noise,

Monalisa shuns Hakeem to keep silent,

Monalisa glance to the the front of the building from the
edge

we cut to see captain Macaulay in curiousity,on glancing at
the dead soliders

He immediately rush inside the house

We cut back to see Monalisa dragging Hakeem hands along as
they head to the Mercedes Benz

                        MONALISA
          can you drive?

                        HAKEEM
          only a bicycle

                        MONALISA
          This is not a joke,can you drive a
          car?

                        HAKEEM
                   (pointing at the bicycle at the far
                   corner)
          I can ride only a bicycle

 Monalisa sighs in distress

                                        CUT TO:
                                        INT.ROOM.GENERA
                                        L BASSEY'S
                                        BASE.CONTINUOUS

we focus on general bassey corpse on the bed

Captain Macualay enters and sight the dead body,

He taps it and groan in anger and dash out of the room

CUT TO:

EXT.ROAD.NIGHT

we focus on Monalisa holding on to Hakeem peddling his
bicycle,on the lonely road surrounded by thick forestation

Soon we see a headlight of an approaching car toward them

> MONALISA
> (Nervous)
> peddle faster

Hakeem peddling fiercely,

Mercedes Benz catch up with and ambush them

We focus on Monalisa and Hakeem in panic watching on

We see captain Macaulay alight from the car,

> CAPTAIN MACAULAY
> (Sit on the car bonnet)
> wow, ridiculous, running away in a
> bicycle,so funny huh,

We focus on Hakeem and Monalisa in great fear

> CAPTAIN MACAULAY
> (Pull out a pistol,point to hakeem)
> Wow,you think you can kill a great
> general,and go have a perfect life
> together right,wow!,what a perfect
> love story,but sadly,the love story
> only have sad ending

We focus on captain macaulay pulling the trigger, gunshot

Focus on Monalisa dropping dead to the groun

We see Hakeem still fear,crying, surrendering

Captain Macaulay pulls the trigger to shoot Hakeem,no bullet

He throws the gun away aggressively

we see hakeem attacking him and engaging in serious
combat,till Hakeem kills captain macaulay

     90.

Hakeem very weak,crawl to Monalisa corpse,crying
He lays on ground beside her

Overhead shot to show Hakeem laying on the ground staring at
the sky, Monalisa and captain macualay corpse laying on the
ground

                    OLDMAN(O.S)
          And that how the love story ends,you
          see obsession is a symptom of true
          love,when you fall love,you get
          obsession,that you can do without the
          person....
                                             CUT TO:

INT.MUDHUT.FOREST.NIGHT

we transition, to the oldman sitting facing felix who is
sitting beside him on the bed

                    OLDMAN
          obsession is what keep love
          burning,me being obsess with the
          forest have kept here for long and
          not wanting to leave,

                    FELIX
          were you also obsess with something?

                    OLDMAN
          What is that?

                    FELIX
              (point to the potrait on the wall)
          Her potrait,you were also obsess with
          it,that you kept it for long

We focus on the oldman smiling,he stand up,pick up the
lantern and walking out of the hut

We focus on Felix watching him

                                             CUT TO:

INT.ROAD.NIGHT

We see Felix in his car,

He dials a call on phone

                    FELIX
              (phone call)
          hello,Joan,can we talk thing out!